RABBIT HAS
A BUSY DAY

RABBIT HAS
A BUSY DAY

A. A. MILNE

illustrated by

ERNEST H. SHEPARD

RABBIT HAS
A BUSY DAY

It was going to be one of Rabbit's busy
days. As soon as he woke up he felt
important, as if everything depended
upon him. It was just the day for
Organizing Something, or for Writing a
Notice Signed Rabbit, or for Seeing What
Everybody Else Thought About It. It was
a perfect morning for hurrying round to
Pooh, and saying, 'Very well, then, I'll tell
Piglet,' and then going to Piglet, and

saying, 'Pooh thinks — but perhaps I'd better see Owl first.' It was a Captainish sort of day, when everybody said 'Yes, Rabbit' and 'No, Rabbit ' and waited until he had told them.

He came out of his house and sniffed the warm spring morning as he wondered what he would do. Kanga's house was nearest, and at Kanga's house was Roo, who said 'Yes, Rabbit' and 'No, Rabbit' almost better than anybody else in the Forest; but there was another animal there nowadays, the strange and Bouncy Tigger; and he was the sort of Tigger who was always in front when you were showing him the way anywhere, and was generally out of sight when at last you came to the place and said proudly 'Here we are!'

'No, not Kanga's,' said Rabbit thoughtfully to himself, as he curled his whiskers in the sun; and, to make quite

sure that he wasn't going there, he turned
to the left and trotted off in the other
direction, which was the way to
Christopher Robin's house.

'After all,' said Rabbit to himself,
'Christopher Robin depends on Me. He's
fond of Pooh and Piglet and Eeyore, and
so am I, but they haven't any Brain. Not
to notice. And he respects Owl, because

you can't help respecting anybody who can spell TUESDAY, even if he doesn't spell it right; but spelling isn't everything. There are days when spelling Tuesday simply doesn't count. And Kanga is too busy looking after Roo, and Roo is too young and Tigger is too bouncy to be of any help, so there's really nobody but Me, when you come to look at it. I'll go and see if there's anything he wants doing, and then I'll do it for him. It's just the day for doing things.'

He trotted along happily, and by-and-by he crossed the stream and came to the place where his friends-and-relations lived. There seemed to be even more of them about than usual this morning, and having nodded to a hedgehog or two, with whom he was too busy to shake hands, and having said, 'Good morning, good morning,' importantly to some of the others, and 'Ah, there you are,' kindly, to the smaller ones, he waved a paw at them over his shoulder, and was gone; leaving such an air of excitement and I-don't-know-what behind him, that several members of the Beetle family, including Henry Rush, made their way at once to the Hundred Acre Wood and began climbing trees, in the hope of getting to the top before it happened, whatever it was, so that they might see it properly.

Rabbit hurried on by the edge of the Hundred Acre Wood, feeling more important every minute, and soon he came to the tree where Christopher Robin lived. He knocked at the door, and he called out once or twice, and then he walked back a little way and put his paw up to keep the sun out, and called to the top of the tree, and then he turned all round and shouted 'Hallo!' and 'I say!' 'It's Rabbit!' — but nothing happened.

Then he stopped and listened, and
everything stopped and listened with
him, and the Forest was very lone and still
and peaceful in the sunshine, until
suddenly a hundred miles above him a
lark began to sing.

'Bother!' said Rabbit. 'He's gone out.'

He went back to the green front door,
just to make sure, and he was turning
away, feeling that his morning had got all
spoilt, when he saw a piece of paper on
the ground. And there was a pin in it, as
if it had fallen off the door.

'Ha!' said Rabbit, feeling quite happy
again. 'Another notice!'

This is what it said:

> GON OUT
> BACKSON
> BISY
> BACKSON
> C.R.

'Ha!' said Rabbit again. 'I must tell the others.' And he hurried off importantly.

The nearest house was Owl's, and to Owl's House in the Hundred Acre Wood he made his way. He came to Owl's door, and he knocked and he rang, and he rang and he knocked, and at last Owl's head came out and said 'Go away, I'm thinking — oh, it's you?' which was how he always began.

'Owl,' said Rabbit shortly, 'you and I have brains. The others have fluff. If there is any thinking to be done in this Forest — and when I say thinking I mean *thinking* — you and I must do it.'

'Yes,' said Owl. 'I was.'

'Read that.'

Owl took Christopher Robin's notice from Rabbit and looked at it nervously. He could spell his own name WOL, and he could spell Tuesday so that you knew it wasn't Wednesday, and he could read quite comfortably when you weren't looking over his shoulder and saying 'Well?' all the time, and he could —

'Well?' said Rabbit.

'Yes,' said Owl, looking Wise and Thoughtful. 'I see what you mean. Undoubtedly.'

'Well?'

'Exactly,' said Owl. 'Precisely.' And he added, after a little thought, 'If you had

not come to me, I should have come to you.'

'Why?' asked Rabbit.

'For that very reason,' said Owl, hoping that something helpful would happen soon.

'Yesterday morning,' said Rabbit solemnly, 'I went to see Christopher Robin. He was out. Pinned on his door was a notice!'

'The same notice?'

'A different one. But the meaning was the same. It's very odd.'

'Amazing,' said Owl, looking at the notice again, and getting, just for a moment, a curious sort of feeling that something had happened to Christopher Robin's back. 'What did you do?'

'Nothing.'

'The best thing,' said Owl wisely.

'Well?' said Rabbit again, as Owl knew he was going to.

'Exactly,' said Owl.

For a little while he couldn't think of anything more; and then, all of a sudden, he had an idea.

'Tell me, Rabbit,' he said, 'the *exact* words of the first notice. This is very important. Everything depends on this. The *exact* words of the *first* notice.'

'It was just the same as that one really.'

Owl looked at him, and wondered whether to push him off the tree; but, feeling that he could always do it afterwards, he tried once more to find out

what they were talking about.

'The exact words, please,' he said, as if Rabbit hadn't spoken.

'It just said, "Gon out. Backson." Same as this, only this says "Bisy Backson" too.'

Owl gave a great sigh of relief.

'Ah!' said Owl. '*Now* we know where we are.'

'Yes, but where's Christopher Robin?' said Rabbit. 'That's the point.'

Owl looked at the notice again. To one of his education the reading of it was easy. 'Gon out, Backson. Bisy, Backson' — just the sort of thing you'd expect to see on a notice.

'It is quite clear what has happened, my dear Rabbit,' he said. 'Christopher Robin has gone out somewhere with Backson. He and Backson are busy together. Have you seen a Backson anywhere about in the Forest lately?'

'I don't know,' said Rabbit. 'That's what I came to ask you. What are they like?'

'Well,' said Owl, 'the Spotted or Herbaceous Backson is just a —'

'At least,' he said, 'it's really more of a —'

'Of course,' he said, 'it depends on the —'

'Well,' said Owl, 'the fact is,' he said, 'I don't know *what* they're like,' said Owl frankly.

'Thank you,' said Rabbit. And he hurried off to see Pooh.

Before he had gone very far he heard a noise. So he stopped and listened. This was the noise:

NOISE, BY POOH

Oh, the butterflies are flying,
Now the winter days are dying,
And the primroses are trying
    To be seen.
And the turtle-doves are cooing,
And the woods are up and doing,
For the violets are blue-ing
    In the green.

Oh, the honey-bees are gumming
On their little wings, and humming
That the summer, which is coming,
    Will be fun.
And the cows are almost cooing,
And the turtle-doves are mooing,
Which is why a Pooh is poohing
    In the sun.

For the spring is really springing;
You can see a skylark singing,
And the blue-bells, which are ringing,
    Can be heard.
And the cuckoo isn't cooing,
But he's cucking and he's ooing,
And a Pooh is simply poohing
    Like a bird.

'Hallo, Pooh,' said Rabbit.

'Hallo, Rabbit,' said Pooh dreamily.

'Did you make that song up?'

'Well, I sort of made it up,' said Pooh.
'It isn't Brain,' he went on humbly,
'because You Know Why, Rabbit; but it
comes to me sometimes.'

'Ah!' said Rabbit, who never let things
come to him, but always went and fetched
them. 'Well, the point is, have you seen a
Spotted or Herbaceous Backson in the
Forest, at all?'

'No,' said Pooh. 'Not a — no,' said
Pooh. 'I saw Tigger just now.'

'That's no good.'

'No,' said Pooh. 'I thought it wasn't.'

'Have you seen Piglet?'

'Yes,' said Pooh. 'I suppose *that* isn't
any good either?' he asked meekly.

'Well, it depends if he saw anything.'

'He saw me,' said Pooh.

Rabbit sat down on the ground next to
Pooh, and, feeling much less important
like that, stood up again.

'What it all comes to is this,' he said.
*'What does Christopher Robin do in the
morning nowadays?'*

'What sort of thing?'

'Well, can you tell me anything you've
seen him do in the morning? These last
few days.'

'Yes,' said Pooh. 'We had breakfast
together yesterday. By the Pine Trees.
I'd made up a little basket, just a little,

fair-sized basket, an ordinary biggish sort
of basket, full of —'

   'Yes, yes,' said Rabbit, 'but I mean later
than that. Have you seen him between
eleven and twelve?'
   'Well,' said Pooh, 'at eleven o'clock — at
eleven o'clock — well, at eleven o'clock,

you see, I generally get home about then. Because I have One or Two Things to Do.'

'Quarter past eleven, then?'

'Well — ' said Pooh.

'Half past?'

'Yes,' said Pooh. 'At half past — or perhaps later — I might see him.'

And now that he did think of it, he began to remember that he *hadn't* seen

Christopher Robin about so much lately. Not in the mornings. Afternoons, yes; evenings, yes; before breakfast, yes; just after breakfast, yes. And then, perhaps, 'See you again, Pooh,' and off he'd go.

'That's just it,' said Rabbit. 'Where?'

'Perhaps he's looking for something.'

'What?' asked Rabbit.

'That's just what I was going to say,' said Pooh. And then he added, 'Perhaps he's looking for a — for a —'

'A Spotted or Herbaceous Backson?'

'Yes,' said Pooh. 'One of those. In case it isn't.'

Rabbit looked at him severely.

'I don't think you're helping,' he said.

'No,' said Pooh. 'I do try,' he added humbly.

Rabbit thanked him for trying, and said that he would now go and see Eeyore, and Pooh could walk with him if he liked. But Pooh, who felt another verse of his song

coming on him, said he would wait for
Piglet, good-bye, Rabbit; so Rabbit went
off.

But, as it happened, it was Rabbit who
saw Piglet first. Piglet had got up early
that morning to pick himself a bunch of
violets; and when he had picked them
and put them in a pot in the middle of his
house, it suddenly came over him that
nobody had ever picked Eeyore a bunch
of violets, and the more he thought of
this, the more he thought how sad it was
to be an Animal who had never had a
bunch of violets picked for him. So he
hurried out again, saying to himself,

'Eeyore, Violets' and then 'Violets, Eeyore,' in case he forgot, because it was that sort of day, and he picked a large bunch and trotted along, smelling them, and feeling very happy, until he came to the place where Eeyore was.

'Oh, Eeyore,' began Piglet a little nervously, because Eeyore was busy.

Eeyore put out a paw and waved him away.

'To-morrow,' said Eeyore. 'Or the next day.'

Piglet came a little closer to see what it was. Eeyore had three sticks on the ground, and was looking at them. Two of the sticks were touching at one end, but not at the other, and the third stick was laid across them. Piglet thought that perhaps it was a Trap of some kind.

'Oh, Eeyore,' he began again, 'I just —'

'Is that little Piglet?' said Eeyore, still looking hard at his sticks.

'Yes, Eeyore, and I —'

'Do you know what this is?'

'No,' said Piglet.

'It's an A.'

'Oh,' said Piglet.

'Not O — A,' said Eeyore severely. 'Can't you *hear*, or do you think you have more education than Christopher Robin?'

'Yes,' said Piglet. 'No,' said Piglet very quickly. And he came closer still.

'Christopher Robin said it was an A, and an A it is — until somebody treads on it,' Eeyore added sternly.

Piglet jumped backwards hurriedly, and smelt at his violets.

'Do you know what A means, little Piglet?'

'No, Eeyore, I don't.'

'It means Learning, it means Education, it means all the things that you and Pooh haven't got. That's what A means.'

'Oh,' said Piglet again. 'I mean, does it?' he explained quickly.

'I'm telling you. People come and go in this Forest, and they say, "It's only Eeyore, so it doesn't count." They walk to and fro saying "Ha ha!" But do they know anything about A? They don't. It's just three sticks to *them*. But to the Educated — mark this, little Piglet — to the Educated, not meaning Poohs and Piglets, it's a great and glorious A. Not,' he added, 'just something that anybody can come and *breathe* on.'

Piglet stepped back nervously, and looked round for help.

'Here's Rabbit,' he said gladly. 'Hallo, Rabbit.'

Rabbit came up importantly, nodded to Piglet, and said, 'Ah, Eeyore,' in the voice of one who would be saying 'Good-bye' in about two more minutes.

'There's just one thing I wanted to ask you, Eeyore. What happens to Christopher Robin in the mornings nowadays?'

'What's this that I'm looking at?' said Eeyore still looking at it.

'Three sticks,' said Rabbit promptly.

'You see?' said Eeyore to Piglet. He turned to Rabbit. 'I will now answer your question,' he said solemnly.

'Thank you,' said Rabbit.

'What does Christopher Robin do in the mornings? He learns. He becomes Educated. He instigorates — I *think* that is the word he mentioned, but I may be referring to something else — he instigorates Knowledge. In my small way I also, if I have the word right, am — am doing what he does. That, for instance, is —'

'An A,' said Rabbit, 'but not a very good

one. Well, I must get back and tell the others.'

Eeyore looked at his sticks and then he looked at Piglet.

'What did Rabbit say it was?' he asked.

'An A,' said Piglet.

'Did you tell him?'

'No, Eeyore, I didn't. I expect he just knew.'

'He *knew*? You mean this A thing is a thing *Rabbit* knew?'

'Yes, Eeyore. He's clever, Rabbit is.'

'Clever!' said Eeyore scornfully, putting a foot heavily on his three sticks. 'Education!' said Eeyore bitterly, jumping on his six sticks. 'What *is* Learning?' asked Eeyore as he kicked his twelve sticks into the air. 'A thing *Rabbit* knows! Ha!'

'I think — ' began Piglet nervously.

'Don't,' said Eeyore.

'I think *Violets* are rather nice,' said Piglet. And he laid his bunch in front of Eeyore and scampered off.

Next morning the notice on Christopher Robin's door said:

GONE OUT
BACK SOON
C.R.

Which is why all the animals in the Forest — except, of course, the Spotted and Herbaceous Backson — now know what Christopher Robin does in the mornings.

Rabbit Has a Busy Day
is taken from *The House at Pooh Corner*
originally published in
Great Britain 11 October 1928
by Methuen & Co. Ltd
Text by A.A. Milne and line drawings by Ernest H. Shepard
copyright under the Berne Convention

This book club edition published by Grolier 1995
Published by arrangement with Reed Children's Books

First published in this edition 1991
by Methuen Children's Books
an imprint of Reed Children's Books
Michelin House, 81 Fulham Road, London SW3 6RB
and Auckland, Melbourne, Singapore and Toronto
Reprinted 1992, 1994, 1995

Printed in Hong Kong

ISBN 0 416 17152 4